RICHARD SCARRY'S
Christmas
Mice

A GOLDEN BOOK • NEW YORK
Western Publishing Company, Inc., Racine, Wisconsin 53404

Formerly Titled CHRISTMAS PRESENT BOOK and THE SANTA CLAUS BOOK

It was early
Christmas morning.

Santa had come
in the night and
left presents
for everyone.

No one was awake yet, except for two little mice.

They climbed up the
Christmas tree to look
at the ornaments.

They looked at the Christmas candies on the shelf.

R

IS FOR REINDEER

Then they looked under the tree.
Santa had put a picture book there...

S IS FOR SLEIGH

...and a castle with soldiers...

...and a blue dollhouse...

...and a bright-red racing car.

There were cookies
and gingerbread.

There was even a gingerbread house.

Santa had not forgotten
to leave two dolls, one large
and one small...

...and lots of cuddly toy animals.

There were presents for everyone,
wrapped in pretty papers and ribbons.

And there was a real, live puppy for the whole family.

But had Santa forgotten the two little mice?

No—he had left them a big piece
of cheese. Merry Christmas, little mice!